THE BABY
BEAST

For Juno

American edition published in 2019 by Andersen Press USA,

an imprint of Andersen Press Ltd.

www.andersenpressusa.com

First published in Great Britain in 2019 by Andersen Press Ltd.,

20 Vauxhall Bridge Road, London SW1V 2SA.

Copyright © Chris Judge, 2019

Distributed in the United States and Canada by

Lerner Publishing Group, Inc.

241 First Avenue North

Minneapolis, MN 55401 USA

For reading levels and more information, look up this title at www.lernerbooks.com.

Printed and bound in Malaysia by Tien Wah Press.

Library of Congress Cataloging-in-Publication Data Available

ISBN: 978-1-5415-5512-9

eBook ISBN: 978-1-5415-6054-3

1-TWP-12/1/18

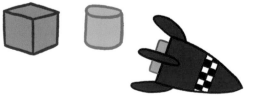

THE BABY
BEAST

CHRIS JUDGE

Ⓐ
Andersen Press USA

One fine, spring morning, the Beast opened his front door to get his newspaper . . .

. . . but discovered a surprise waiting for him. It looked like an egg. The Beast had never been given an egg before.

"How do you look after an egg?" the Beast wondered.

First he tried sharing some of his breakfast.

Then he took it for a nice long walk.

But the egg didn't seem to be enjoying itself at all.

Doing his chores, the Beast forgot about the egg . . .

. . . and lost it!   Almost.

When someone knocked on the door during
bath time, the Beast forgot about the egg again . . .

. . . and dropped it! (Ouch.)

He really was awful at looking after eggs. To show he was sorry, the Beast took the egg on a hike up his favorite mountain.

But when he stopped for lunch, things did not go according to plan.

It rolled right into the emergency room.
Luckily, Dr. Yoko was an expert on eggs.*

*Officially called an eggspert.

"You must follow these instructions," said
Dr. Yoko. "You won't have to wait long."

The Beast read the instructions carefully.

LOOKING AFTER

1. Keep it warm
- Turn up the heat
- Egg needs to be wrapped up
- Nest needs to be snuggly and soft

2. Turn your egg
Turn your egg every four hours to make sure it is heated evenly.

YOUR FIRST EGG

3. Play soft music (nothing too loud)

4. Give it lots of love

5. Wait

It all seemed clear except for one thing: "What am I waiting for?" wondered the Beast.

The Beast bought all the things he would need,
plus some things he wouldn't . . .

Then he carried all his new things home.

When everything was ready, the
only thing left to do was wait.
(It had been a long day.)

WHAT TO
EXPECT
WHEN
YOU'RE
EGG-
SPECTING

The next morning, the Beast opened his shed door to see the egg and got a nasty surprise. The shed had been burgled!

"Oh, Egg!" sobbed the Beast. "You were heavy and you were hard work and you were often incredibly annoying, but I loved you."

And that was when something wonderful happened.

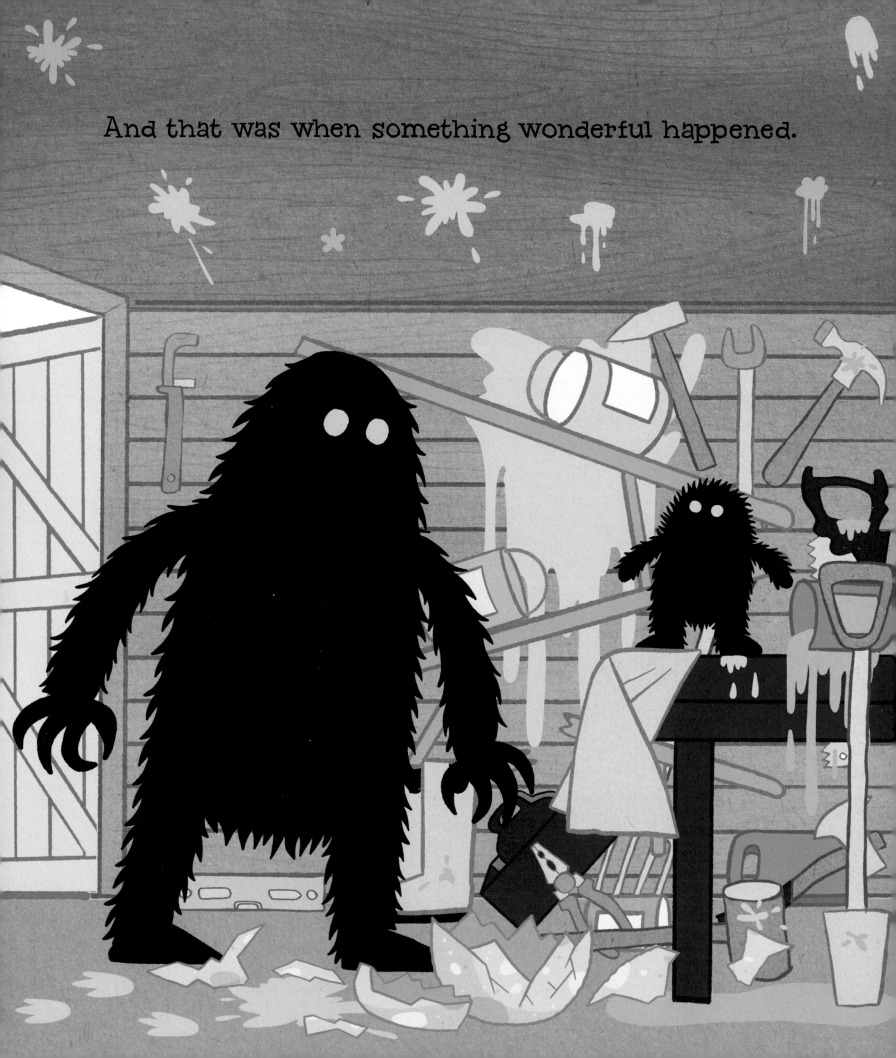

The Beast realized what (or rather, who) he had been waiting for.

Dr. Yoko was very pleased. The Beast had done a wonderful job. Now instead of a list of instructions, she gave him a whole book to learn how to look after Baby Beast.

At first it seemed like really hard work,
and the Beast had a few setbacks.

But after a while,

he seemed to get the hang of it.

The Beast's favorite time was the end of the day, because they both loved bedtime stories.

"Good night, sleep tight Baby Beast," he whispered, thinking how sometimes, the biggest surprises are the best.